Jon Scieszka's
TRUCKTOWN

Gabriella Garbage Truck

Rescue Rita

Dump Truck Dan

Payloader Pete

Jack Truck

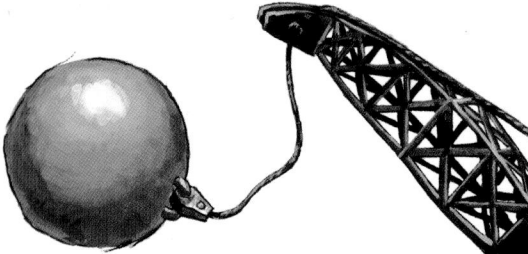

Wrecking Crane Rosie

Cement Mixer Melvin

Big Rig

Grader Kat

Monster Truck Max

Pumper Pat   Hook and Ladder Lucy

Izzy Ice Cream Truck

Tow Truck Ted

SIMON AND SCHUSTER
First published in Great Britain in 2009 by Simon and Schuster UK Ltd
1st Floor, 222 Gray's Inn Road, London WC1X 8HB
A CBS Company

Originally published in 2008 by Simon and Schuster Books for Young Readers,
an imprint of Simon & Schuster Children's Publishing Division, New York

Book design by Dan Potash
A CIP catalogue record for this book is
available from the British Library upon request

ISBN: 978 1 84738 507 9

Printed in China

1 3 5 7 9 10 8 6 4 2

Characters and environments developed by the

DESIGN
garage

David Shannon • Loren Long • David Gordon

ILLUSTRATION CREW

Drawings by
Juan Pablo Navas

Colour by
Isabel Nadal

Executive Producer
TOT
INDUSTRIES

in association with
ANIMAGIC S. L.

Creative Supervisor
Sergio Pablos

Art Director
Dan Potash

SIMON AND SCHUSTER
LONDON ○ NEW YORK ○ SYDNEY

To Justin, because
he always tries
- JS

Melvin might?

written by

Jon Scieszka

Cement Mixer Melvin worries.

Melvin worries, "I might get dirty."

Melvin worries, "I might get stuck."

"Come on, Melvin," says Jack. "The bridge isn't finished. But we've found a great new way to get across."

This worries Melvin even more.

"First you ROAR!" says Pete.
Pete roars down the hill.

"Me too," beeps Rita. Rita roars down the hill.

"Oh, no," says Melvin. "I can't try that."

"Then you **SOAR!**" yells Pete.
Pete soars through the air.

"**Me too,**" beeps Rita.
Rita soars through the air.

"Oh, no," says Melvin.
"I can't try that."

Jack says, "Come on, Melvin. Follow me!"

"Oh, no!" worries Melvin.
"I can't try any of that."

"HELP!",

beeps Rita.

"Yes, I need help," says Melvin.

Melvin sees that Rita really
needs help.

But Jack and Pete are gone.

"But I'm worried I can't."

"Maybe I can try."

Melvin **ROARS** down the hill.

Melvin **SOARS** through the air.

But he gives Rita a push.

"I can try."

"I can try."

"I can try."

Melvin saves Rita with one big . . .

Jack and Pete come racing back.
"Melvin!" honks Pete. "You did it!"

"You roared! You soared!
You really splashed!"
says Jack.

"I know," says Melvin . . .

"… but I think I might still worry."

"Me too," beeps Rita.

And Rita and Melvin drive slowly home.

"Let me tell you something."

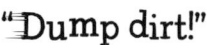

"Dump dirt!"

"Me too!?"

"Heh, heh, heh."

"Follow me!"

"WHAM! Oops."

"I might be worried."

"Out of my way."

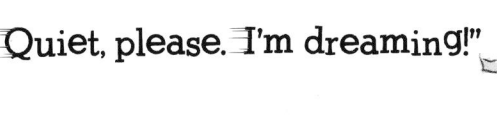

"Rules are . . .

. . . rules."

"To the MAX!"

"Do you want an ice cream?
Do you want an ice cream?
Do you want an ice cream?"

"I have a plan."